brothers

FLUB

ELIMINÉ

Scared Stiff

Adapted by **Paul Christian**
Based on the script by **David Burke**
Created by **David Burke** and **Laslo Nosek**
Story Edited by **Tom Mason** and **Dan Danko**

Special thanks to **Glenn R. Hendricks**

ST-ISIDORE/PLANTAGENET-SUD

IP007416

™ and ©                                                    d.

All rights reserved. No part of this book may be reproduced or utilized in any form or
by any means, electronic or mechanical, including photocopying, recording, or by any
information storage and retrieval system, without written permission from the publisher.
Printed in the United States of America.    ISBN 0-8167-6855-2
10 9 8 7 6 5 4 3 2 1

Fraz and Guapo, the Brothers Flub, were chowing down on some Chinese food with their friends Valerina and Squeege.

"That was positively deee-licious," said Fraz. "I love making deliveries to the Land of Really Great Chinese Food!"

"How right you are, Fraz," said Guapo, burping loudly. "And now, my favorite part . . . fortune cookies!"

Everyone grabbed a fortune cookie.
"'Your hairstyle will come back into fashion—maybe,'" sighed Valerina.
"'You will be the master of space and time,'"read Squeege. "Cool!"

"'You will have a rich, happy life, and a large ham will fall in your lap,'" read Guapo.

"'You are doomed,'" read Fraz calmly. "Doomed. Not bad. Who would have thought . . . Aaahhh!" Fraz slumped in his seat. "Oh, woe is me! Woe *couldn't* be more me!"

"Don't worry, Fraz," said Guapo kindly. "These fortunes never come true!"

Just then a large ham fell into Guapo's lap.

Fraz was really nervous now. "Doom could strike at any moment!" he cried.

"Come on, Fraz," said Guapo. "That silly fortune is no reason to be scared of every little thing."

"Maybe you're right," said Fraz, feeling a little better.
A loud noise interrupted the brothers as a giant steel ball crashed
through the door and rolled across the room, flattening Fraz.
"Oh, no," moaned Fraz. "I'm definitely doomed!"

Mizz Boomdeeyay pulled up on her scooter. She screeched to a halt next to the brothers.

"Listen up, you poisonous little shank-brained mealy worms!" she shouted. "Some wacko needs that ball for his oversized pinball machine. You two little lumps of dumbness must deliver it to the City of Oversized Games. Now get going! Time is money—my money!"

The Brothers Flub raced onto the *Hoog*, their delivery ship.
"How's our beloved cargo, Fraz?" called Guapo from the cockpit.
Fraz was too busy examining the pinball to answer.
"You can't fool me," Fraz hissed at the pinball. "I know all your
shiny doom-ball tricks. I know you were sent here to destroy me!"

Fraz pushed a button on the wall. "I'll show you who's boss, you round rolling demon!" he shouted. The rear door opened, and the ball went flying into space.

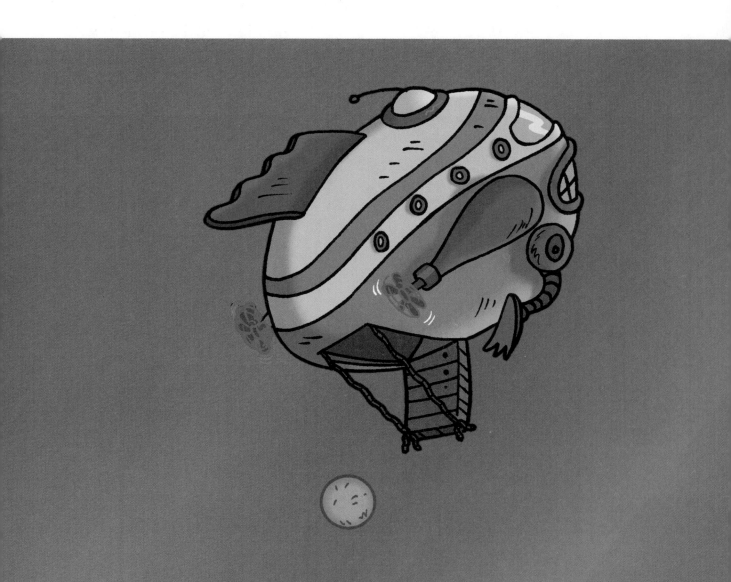

"Fraz!" called Guapo, walking into the cargo hold. "How is our precious pinball?"

"Umm, fine, just fine," said Fraz, smiling nervously.

Guapo looked around curiously. "So where is it?" he asked.

"I did what I had to do!" Fraz wailed, pointing at the open door. "It was either the ball or me! I was doomed!"

Guapo looked at his brother as a handy book dropped down.
"Don't worry, Fraz-o," he said, glancing at the book. "We'll replace
the pinball with a giant metal pigeon egg from the Land of Giant
Metal Pigeons. Our client will never know the difference!"

In no time, the brothers arrived in the Land of Giant Metal Pigeons. They peered through the porthole at a mother pigeon guarding its giant metal egg.

"Great Mother of Doom!" shouted Fraz. "Guapo, that's no pigeon, that's the Pigeonator! How will we ever get that egg away from her?"

"I'm glad you asked," said Guapo, smiling. He took off his boot.

A few moments later, Fraz was being lowered from the *Hoog,* holding Guapo's smelly sock in a sealed tube. When he got near the pigeon, Fraz opened the tube.

A horrible smell filled the air, chasing the pigeon away. Fraz grabbed the egg, and Guapo steered the *Hoog* toward the City of Oversized Games.

"Bee-jabbers!" exclaimed Guapo as they neared their destination. "Look at the games!"

Guapo headed over to the Vidivici Pinball Arcade, with Fraz still hanging on to the egg.

A man in a suit was waiting for them. "You got my pinball?" he asked gruffly.

"Yes, Mr. Vidivici!" said Guapo. "Here it is!"

Mr. Vidivici walked over to the egg, inspecting it. "This isn't a pinball," he growled. Then he jabbed his finger into Guapo. "When Vinnie Vidivici orders a giant pinball, he expects a giant pinball!"

With another jab of his finger, Mr. Vidivici sent Guapo backward over the platform. Fraz screamed as Guapo landed in the giant pinball machine.

Guapo began to roll like a ball and bounce off the bumpers.

"Weeee! Yowza!" he shouted gleefully. The crowd around the pinball machine cheered. "This is great!"

Fraz nervously watched his brother from the platform. "Guapo's getting pulverized!" he said. "Somebody's got to save him."

"Your brother is putting up quite a fight," said Mr. Vidivici. Suddenly, a giant pinball rolled out of nowhere and headed right toward Guapo. Mr. Vidivici grinned wickedly. "But the ball always wins!"

"That's it!" shouted Fraz, striking a heroic pose. "I don't care what the fortune cookie says. I've got to save my brother!"

Fraz leaped off the platform and into the giant game. A pinball squashed him immediately. Fraz got up and fought his way through the game to Guapo. Then he grabbed his brother and jumped out of the pinball machine.

"Game over!" Fraz shouted. The crowd went wild.

Guapo turned to Fraz. "Thanks for saving me and all, but I was having fun."

Fraz's jaw dropped. "So . . . so I did that for nothing?"

"What do you mean, nothing?" said Guapo. "You got over being afraid, didn't you?"

"Oh, sure, throw that in my face," Fraz huffed.

Just then, Mr. Vidivici showed up, pushing the giant pigeon egg. "You two guys put on a good show. Now get rid of this thing and get me my pinball!"

Fraz stood up tall. "I'm not afraid of you," he said. "And I'm not afraid of the ball of doom or this stupid egg . . ."

Suddenly, the egg began to crack. Out stepped a giant metal pigeon.
"But I *am* afraid of this pigeon!" Fraz screamed. The baby pigeon
picked up both brothers and took off.

"Hey," said Guapo, as he and Fraz were whisked away, "if we ask nicely, maybe the pigeon will take us to the Land of Shiny Giant Pinballs."

It was just another wacky day in the life of the Brothers Flub!